Babushka's Doll

To Lauren Estelle Washington

Babushka's Doll

Patricia Polacco

HOUGHTON MIFFLIN COMPANY

BOSTON

ATLANTA   DALLAS   GENEVA, ILLINOIS   PALO ALTO   PRINCETON

It wasn't that Natasha was a truly naughty child. She just never understood why she had to wait for things.

"Babushka," Natasha said, for in Russian, Babushka means "grandmother." "Please stop doing the laundry and push me in the swing."

"My darling child," Babushka said. "I have to do the laundry first. Would you like to help me?"

"No," said Natasha. "I want to swing now."

5

"Aren't you finished yet? I want to go for a ride in the goat cart."

"My precious," Babushka said. "I must hang up these clothes while the sun is shining."

"But the sun will be shining all day. I want to go now, Babushka. Take me."

Babushka went to feed the goats. Natasha followed.
"But I'm hungry, too, Babushka. My stomach is making
noises. I want to eat now."
"Don't be selfish, darling," said Babushka. "These poor
creatures need to be fed. They cannot fix their own lunch."

"Now I am finished," said Babushka, "and now we will have lunch." She took a kettle down from a high shelf.

Natasha looked up on the shelf where the kettle had been, and there was a little doll she had never seen before.

"Is that your doll, Babushka?" she asked.

"Yes, dear, it was my doll when I was a little girl like you."

"Did you play with her all the time?" asked Natasha.

"No, my dear, I played with her only once. Only once."

"I have finished my soup now," said Natasha. "May I hold the little doll? Just for a little while?"

Babushka got the doll down from the high shelf. "Yes, it is just the right time for you to play with her," said Babushka. She handed the doll to Natasha. "I am going to the store for groceries," she said. "You may play with the doll until I get back."

As soon as the door closed behind Natasha's grandmother, something happened. The little doll began to move. She jumped to her feet and did a little dance. For a moment, Natasha was a bit frightened. But then the doll called, "Come on, Tasha. Let's go out and play."

Natasha and the doll ran and ran…until Natasha could run
no more. As soon as Natasha sat down to catch her breath,
the doll said, "Get up, Tasha. You get up now! I want to play."

"I'll swing you on the swing," Natasha said.

"*Wheeee!*" the doll squealed. "Push harder. I want to go higher."

Natasha pushed the doll higher and higher. But soon she grew tired.

"Don't stop, Tasha," cried the doll. "Don't stop. I want you to swing me higher."

"I'll take you for a ride in the goat cart," Natasha said.

"Oh, goody, Tasha," the doll chirped. "And don't you slow down. You better keep going as long as I want. Do you hear me? As long as I want."

Soon Natasha couldn't lead the goat cart any longer.
"I have to stop," said Natasha. "I need to rest."
"Now I want to eat," said the doll.
Poor Natasha was very tired. But she tried her best to make lunch.

Babushka's doll spilled the tea. She sloshed the soup from her spoon, and she flung noodles over her head. Then she pounded her fist in the mess and laughed and laughed.

Suddenly she stopped laughing
and started to scream.

"My dress, Tasha. It's all dirty.
I want *you* to wash it. You wash
it right now."

Natasha washed the little dress
and hung it on the line.

Then she ironed it
and put it on the doll.

"You didn't do it right," said
the doll. "My dress is all wrinkled."
   Natasha began to cry. "I'm just a
little girl," she said between sobs.
"I wish you were just a doll."

"My darling girl," a voice called out. "Why are you crying, my precious child?"

"Babushka," sobbed Natasha. "Your little doll came to life and she was very naughty. All she wanted me to do was work. She never let me rest. She made me iron her dress and I don't even know how. I'm just a little girl."

"There, there," Babushka said. "You must have had a bad dream."

"Maybe," said Natasha.

Her grandmother smiled and held Natasha closer. "From now on, you can play with the little doll any time you want."

"No, thank you, Babushka," Natasha said. "Once is enough."

Babushka picked up the little doll and put her back on the high shelf. "It looks like you had quite a day," she said softly.

The little doll gave Babushka a wink and went back to being just a doll.

And Natasha turned out to be quite nice after all.